Revival Island

Revival Island

ISBN 979-8-9851873-4-2 (sc print)

ISBN 979-8-9851873-5-9 (ebook)

Printed in the United States of America

Beta Readers and editors: Cathy Foulkes & Janet Pavlons

IngramSparks Publishing (Ingram: Lightning Source, LLC)

One Ingram Blvd., La Vergne, TN 37086

PDW PUBLICATIONS

Revival Island

Kim Foulkes

Contents

Chapter 1

Amalia and Quin

I sat still in the courthouse, feeling nervous and uncomfortable. The regret of screaming and fighting on our last phone conversation hits me. "Why can't we be civil and even talk about the children?"

I really don't want to see my soon-to-be ex, even for a minute. I am praying he doesn't show. I am so grateful I made it to court. I have been counting down the days. I am so glad today is the day that I can finally get free.

My ex walks in; he glares at me. If looks could kill... I don't want to show any fear, so I stare right back. I can be an ass as well. I learned from the best. I am so glad this will be over soon. Then, I can start the relationship that I have on the back burner, just cooking on low, keeping it warm enough that the fire doesn't go completely out. Finally, a decent man who makes a great living is interested in me.

My ex has someone as well. He decided to start that relationship smack in the middle of ours. I was so bitter, but now I don't care. I go back and forth from being happy for them, to feeling sorry for her.

At least we agree on one thing, that we both want the divorce. We have agreed to share custody of our two teenage children. We are even sharing the attorney fees. As I am deep into daydreaming of my new life, beginning with a celebratory massage, the judge interrupts my thoughts.

"Amalia and Quin, please come forward."

Oh yes, here is the moment I have been waiting for. I stand and straighten my new pantsuit.

"Yes, Your Honor."

Quin follows in "Yes, ma'am, I mean, Your Honor."

"Well, after careful consideration and finding no abuse on either part, you both qualify for our newest program, Revival Island. The only requirement is that you complete the course in its entirety. It will be for one week. It's simple, you will be dropped off in a remote part of the island with ten items. If you make it for the full week, without tapping out, then in return you will be granted the divorce and all fees will be paid. Now, how does that sound? Would you like some time to discuss it?"

For me, it was a no-brainer, as I was not sure how I was going to produce my half of the attorney fees. I responded, "Count me in!"

My ex who is the biggest penny pincher I know and who loves a challenge, followed with, "When do we leave, Your Honor?"

We decided on leaving the following Monday. For the five items, I chose a Bible, bear horn, sleeping bag, sunscreen, and a pan. Quin brought soap, a saw, a fishing pole, a lighter, and a tarp. The island is in the Caribbean region, in the remote southwest part. We were told there is fresh water to be found on the island, plenty of trees for wood or to use for shelter, fresh fruit, and of course fish. It didn't seem like this was going to be hard at all. I planned to research ocean vegetation that was edible before leaving. I could lose about ten pounds, so a week without carbs would do me good. I wasn't sure how I would do without coffee though.

We were dropped off with a map of the island, and on it was an arrow pointing to the freshwater supply. We would have to work together to find the water as the map was a little confusing. But in the meantime, we would be fine, as we were surrounded by coconut trees and could drink coconut water. However, for cooking, we needed the fresh water. We decided to make our shelter near the waterfall.

I really cringed at having to look at him or talk at all. I tried my best to just drink in the view. The white sand beach, see-through water, and warm breeze was amazing. I sat down feeling the weight of the world leave me as I got lost in the beauty.

"Hello, Amalia, am I going to have to do everything as usual?!"

My husband's annoying voice quickly snapped me back to reality. Oh great, here we go already, him doing everything?! I have no idea whatsoever what that was supposed to mean, as I ran the household and took care of the children.

"How can I help you my dear?" I responded in the most condescending tone I could muster.

Quin replied, "We need to figure out the map and find the supply of fresh water. It looks like there are three different maps that lead to different treasures. The first one is for water. We need to put our heads together before darkness sets in!"

We sat down on a large rock overlooking the ocean holding the treasure map in hand. The realization that we were alone on this beautiful beach together for seven days hits me. I felt so vulnerable. I had grown independent over the last three years since we separated. I had to learn how to do things myself and be alone. I took care of the yard and did minor repairs to the house. I kept telling myself I didn't need to worry or need him now, either. I could take care of myself here just as well as I did back home. We looked over the map. The picture was leading us away from the shoreline into the forest of trees. We decided to start hiking.

As we got thick into the forest of hills and trees, I made up my mind that no matter what, I would not show any weakness. I was somehow able to push through and keep up with my ex. Suddenly as my legs were starting to ache and cramp up, my ex-yells, "Ami, listen, do you hear that?"

I stopped and listened intently. Ahh, the sound of rushing water. I was overjoyed! We ran over towards the sound and there we found the most beautiful waterfall. It was running over a stream of rocks and had two separate pools of water to the side. We filled our pan with water. As I put it up to my lips, Quin yelled, "Don't drink it yet. We need to boil it to make sure we kill the organisms."

We surveyed the area and found a flat area surrounded by vegetation with two trees a few feet apart. We tied our tarp to the trees creating shelter for us to sleep. The waterfall was in view of our campsite and to the right was a panoramic view of the ocean, so picturesque.

Quin said, "I will be back; stay here. I am going to get wood for a fire."

He handed me the bear horn and told me to use it if anything came near me and then headed off into the trees.

As I sat there waiting, I wondered how we got to this place. I remember the first time we met. I had been out with a group of friends; my friends were completely drunk, out of it, and being so unruly. I was the designated driver and was having trouble getting the two of them into my car so that we could leave. Quin came out of the bar he had been bartending at to pay his way through college. He came to my rescue. He gently picked up my friends one by one getting them in the car. He then offered to come with me to get each of them home, as I would have had to leave them in the car until the next day. I am five feet tall and at the time was barely one hundred pounds.

I was so desperate as it was a wintry night, and it wouldn't be safe to leave them in the car. I said that would be most appreciated. He rode with us and helped them both into their apartments. After I drove him back to his car, I asked if I could take him to dinner the following night to pay him back for the help. He agreed. When it was time to pay the bill, he had already paid. He was such a gentleman and would not hear of a woman paying. He said that was how he was raised. He was brought up by a Southern Baptist mom who loved the Lord and manners, almost equally.

We parted ways, but I could not get him off my mind. We decided if we were meant to be in each other's lives we would somehow find one another again. We lived on opposite sides of town and yet wound up on the same crowded city bus seven months later. We both had car trouble and had vehicles in the shop. We then could not deny that God, the universe, or something wanted us together. We agreed we had to date to find out.

Dating was a complete joy, we laughed more than anything. It was an adventure and a friendship. I was treated with the utmost respect. He opened doors, paid for all dates, and would even trade meals if I liked his better. He always made sure my needs were taken care of first. He had such respect for women and would not even consider having sex until we were married. He believed sex outside of marriage ruined things, accelerated a relationship, and caused confusion. We dated for two years before we were engaged. It was no easy feat, but so worth the wait. Sex was incredible and magical, almost spiritual-like. It was on our wedding night after a tropical wedding in Hawaii with only four of our closest friends. The warmth of the air and the salty smell of the ocean quickly took me back to that place. As I was reminiscing, I realized how darkness had crept in. I started worrying if something had happened to Quin. I held tight to the emergency phone we were given if we needed to leave the island or if anything went horribly wrong. I started yelling his name and worrying what I would tell our kids if he was gone.

He quickly appeared over the hill and was carrying firewood. I was so glad to see him. I ran to him and greeted him happily. His shirt was so wet with sweat, and he had used a lot of energy cutting the wood. I helped him carry the wood and told him he needed to drink water. We quickly got the fire going and boiled the water we had found. After the water cooled, we took turns drinking it.

He fell asleep soon after. The only sleeping bag we had fit two, so he fell asleep next to me. It felt so familiar, his warm body up against mine. I felt safe and protected. He was like a heater, and I was always so cold. He would say we were created for each other. He warmed me up and I cooled him off. My heart suddenly revived for him. It had been dead for years but now miraculously felt alive again. I wondered how that was possible and if he felt the same. I thought back to Dan, the man I had back home. The good guy who was so good he refused to get physical with me until the divorce was final. I thought too about our marriage counselor, who decided that instead of helping us with our marriage she would help herself to my husband. They were engaged now.

We had many great years in the marriage before the tragedy struck that took our sweet baby girl. I drifted off to sleep thinking about all the good times. I was awakened by the sound of splashing water and sat up straight trying to get my bearings back and remember where I was. My ex was swimming near the freshwater that we had found. I quickly made my way over there. I needed to cool off and was so sweaty. I only had my bra and underwear as I had not packed a swimsuit. I didn't want to be wet all day, so I took everything off and walked into the pool of water.

My ex had a bar of soap and was now completely clean. He got out as I got in. His body was so muscular and very nice to look at. I thought of Dan and quickly looked away. I felt guilty seeing him naked as I had a good guy waiting for me back home. And it felt wrong to look, as he wasn't mine to look at anymore. Quin handed me the soap and acted as if he had not even noticed me standing there naked in the crystal-clear water. He walked back to our camp. Boy, he was sure loyal to his fiancé. I felt jealous. I felt robbed. I mean Dan would be great, but would I ever feel again like I felt for Quin? It was true love, at least on my part.

As I got out, Quin was cooking a fish over the fire. The smell was amazing. I was so hungry. He took the smallest piece and gave me the rest. We sat there with nothing to do. I said, "Quin, do you still love me?"

He, taken back, responded, "Ami don't go there, I would rather not say."

"Well, I love you and I always will. Nothing will change that."

"How can you love me, when it's my fault our daughter died?" he responded.

"Your fault, how could it be? If anything, it is mine. I left the candle on. You saved us all. You got her out too but the infection from the burn killed her. Oh Quin, I am so sorry. It is all 'my' fault."

Crying, now I was shaking. I never told him I was sorry. I never took responsibility; I blamed the kids for lighting the candle. I couldn't accept the fact that I had. It took seven years to finally admit it. And all this time he blamed himself. No wonder he pulled away from me immediately after. I was so afraid of what he would say next now that the truth was out.

"I am so sorry; I should have told you the truth sooner. I should have never blamed the boys."

He pulled me close. "Honey, I knew all along you lit the candle. I saw you do it. But it is not your fault, it was an accident. Please don't blame yourself."

Before too long, we were in each other's arms crying softly, grieving for our sweet baby girl. Together we relived her birth and all the memories we had in the four years she was with us. We had always wanted a daughter and had two boys. She was such a gift, an answer to prayer, and our baby, our youngest. We laughed so hard together remembering the funny things she would say. As I lay on his chest, I could feel his heart beating so strong inside of him. I lay still quietly listening to the sound, as warm tears kept falling from our eyes. His embrace and arms felt safe around me. I didn't want him to ever let me go. Why had we never done this? Why did we grieve alone? Why did we allow the accident to not only burn down our house, but our love, our family, and our firm foundation?

After what seemed like forever of peaceful silence, Quin spoke, "Baby I do love you, I never stopped. I just couldn't face you. I believed you would never forgive me for not getting Rachel out fast enough. My fiancé Linda was safe. She knew how to help me heal of the pain. I don't love her the way I love you. I don't. I mean I was hoping it would become like 'our' love. I tried to make it happen, but I couldn't." He went on to say, "Please forgive me for cheating on you, for not being the man you needed and deserved. I am sorry I wasn't man enough to walk through the pain with you."

I told him I had forgiven him and that was the past and over. I explained how God helped me forgive him years ago. I said I wanted good for him, even if it was with her. He gently wiped the tears from my eyes and tilted my chin up. He leaned down ever so slowly, his moist wet lips coming towards mine. My mind went from no we can't do this as it is wrong to oh, please don't stop. The kiss was gentle and soft. It was so full of passion of every kind, familiar, new, pure, erotica, all wrapped together in one. I felt electricity go through my body. My body physically ached for him. I wanted him so badly, like never before. I wanted him as close as I could get him. Before I knew what was happening as his body was wrapped around mine, he slipped inside of me. It was the best feeling ever, it just felt right. I felt so warm all over. It was spectacular. I never wanted this moment to end or to separate from him. We lay there in amazement but also thinking about Linda and Dan.

The remaining week was full of hiking, laughing, and swimming in the ocean. We even forgot to find the other treasures. We watched the sun rise and set holding hands on the beach. We talked all night. We made love day and night.

When our time was over, we were taken into the judge's chamber. The Judge called us to the front. "Well, you have successfully completed the course so here is, as promised, your divorce decree. I have signed it so all that remains is each of your signatures. The attorney's fees have been paid. As soon as the decree reached our hands, my husband took the decree and tore it up in front of the judge. The decision for us was easy. We decided to stay together and start fresh.

> *Two are better than one, for they can help each other succeed. If one person falls, the other can reach out and help. But someone who falls alone is in real trouble. Ecclesiastes 4:9-10 NLT.*

Before we even left the courthouse, we made phone calls to Dan and to Linda ending it. We cut off all ties and contact with them both, deleting their numbers from our phones. We decided at once to move back in together. We were not taking any chances. We called our pastor, making weekly appointments for counseling. For us, Revival Island did what it was supposed to do, "revive." We found out we were part of the twenty percent success rate, so only two out of ten come to this decision.

We were so impressed with the program that we decided to become a part of it. We wanted to get the percentage to double from twenty to forty percent success rate. We propositioned the judge to create an entire team for Revival Island, agreeing we would do the challenging work. The team would come up with ideas on ways to make it a higher success rate. One change was to interview all couples at their departure from the island for feedback, to help determine why it failed some and worked for others. We would add to the program licensed counselors and activities that would draw people together into teamwork. We came up with a plan to recreate first dates on the island. We also will follow up with all the success stories of those who chose to stay together and start a women's and men's support group for them.

We found out the program was started due to the judge's own personal experiences. She had been through multiple divorces and wanted to do something to help give marriages hope. She had witnessed too many heartbreaks and believed many marriages could be saved with a second chance.

As we began our new life together, we were so full of joy. Our love was stronger than ever. We were just so grateful to have each other again and for our family to be whole. Our two teenage sons thrived; their grades even improved, and they both decided to go to college. We got back into the swing of life again and things were looking up. We made our marriage a priority this time around and went on two dates a month. We were in a great place when we received a call that two of our church members had been involved in a fatal accident. The couple had just adopted a four-year girl from Haiti who survived the accident without a scratch. We were asked if we would consider taking care of her until other arrangements could be made. We jumped at the chance and before too long, we had a daughter again.

The redemptive love of Jesus amazes me. He truly does give and takes away, as the Bible says. I still do not understand why we had to lose our precious baby girl, but I know she watches over us, and we will one day see her again. I know that God loves us with a love greater than the vast ocean, which for a week, we called home. God is the restorer of things broken, whether marriages, hearts, or families.

Chapter 2

Nora and Max

It was Tuesday at ten o'clock in the morning when I arrived at court. I tried to look the most beautiful I have ever looked in my life. I had my hair colored an all-over bright blond with golden honey highlights throughout. I had my nails done and was wearing a very expensive navy skirt and cream-colored blouse. I had lost thirty pounds since the separation and had my braces off a week before our court date. I finally had straight teeth and felt, for once in my life, truly confident. I had been to the salon the day before for a natural spray tan. It was a hard, sad day for me, and I wanted to look my best with the hopes that my husband couldn't resist me and would change his mind. I did not want the divorce but agreed to it. I had waited and prayed for two long years that my husband would have a change of heart. I was growing weary and needing closure myself. I could not put my heart on hold much longer. I had three small children to raise who deserved my full attention. As we sat in the tense courtroom, I could not even look at my husband while we waited for the judge to speak.

Tears welled up as I remembered back to the first day I saw my husband. There was a huge lump in my throat as I tried not to cry. I remembered seeing him helping the neighbor lady carry in groceries. She was a widow and had dropped her bag of groceries. He was outside playing basketball with his friends when he noticed her fall and he ran to her aid. I was so curious about this kind, teen boy and watched him for weeks, trying to get up the nerve to introduce myself. I had just moved to town and was homeschooled. I was shy and awkward, I had an overbite and struggled with acne. I was sure he would never even talk to me.

"Nora and Max, please come up to the front. I have read over the paperwork from your attorney. I find your story to be fascinating and I believe there is still hope for this relationship. I would like to offer you a week on Revival Island. If you stay the entire week and you still want the divorce, it will be granted free of charge."

My heart leaped inside of me. I was in complete joy as my hope was suddenly restored.

I yelled, "Sure, I will agree to go!" My husband was stoic, but he was a believer in destiny and agreed to go as well.

He responded, "Your Honor, I will go and give it my all."

We left the very next day. We both wanted this over with, but for very different reasons. I wanted a chance to win him back to start our life together again. He wanted closure and a divorce. I packed my items. I brought perfume, a black negligee, my red silk comforter, a pitcher with a built-in filtering system, and a cooking pot. My husband packed, a tent, fishing net, panic alarm, a knife, and a fire starter.

We arrived by helicopter on the island. As they were ascending away, I felt such elation. This was a dream come true to have seven days alone with my husband. I had been begging my husband for even a weekend away together, which he always refused. My husband looked sad, but he almost looked hopeful as well.

We were dropped off near the freshwater supply. The view was stunning. The rolling water was streaming over huge multicolored large stones. The sound of the water falling was calming to my soul. The ocean and white sand beach to our right looked like a painting. It looked too beautiful to be real. We decided before nightfall to search for berries. Max was a Boy Scout leader and a top survival expert. He knew which were edible and which were poisonous. He said he needed some alone time and left for the search. I took a stroll on the beach as I prayed for a miracle.

When my husband came back, he washed the berries and brought them to me. He said he now was going to cut down some firewood. I offered to go with him, but he said he needed me to protect our spot. It seemed to me he was doing everything he could to avoid being around me. He was gone for so long that I became discouraged.

I thought back to what brought us to this place. I remembered back to the moment I broke our marriage vows. We were on a family vacation in a large South Carolina beach house. We were with our two small children, his brother, his parents, and my great aunt. In the middle of the night, the day before the vacation was to end, I drank way too much. I did it purposefully to get my nerve up. Without being drunk, I would never be able to go through with my plan to cheat. Everyone in the house was asleep and I slipped off my clothes and snuck into my brother-in-law's bed. It felt so exciting and risky. It wasn't just a one-time poor judgment. This lust for him had been building up for years, the flirting, the accidental brushing up against me, the stares. One time he bumped into me. I spilled my drink down my front and he used a rag to blot it up right at the table while we all ate. No one batted an eye. Everyone trusted us so much as they knew how much my husband and I were in love. It honestly appeared innocent at first. I really thought that I was imagining things. But then felt a pull towards him and him wanting me and my desire took over. I began daydreaming about making love to him, even while making love to Max. It was so sick, wrong, and sinful. That is how sin creeps in. It starts off small and innocent, but once it takes hold it's hard to turn back. We got away with the affair and both felt sickening remorse. We promised each other to never do it again and we kept that promise. The guilt of it made me a more attentive and better wife. But then three and a half months later, I was throwing up every morning. Panic gripped me as I knew what this meant. A year earlier my husband had a vasectomy, so I had some explaining to do. My brother-in-law begged me to abort our child. He said he could never look his brother in the eye again if I had the baby. I could not kill another human being. I did not feel I had that right. This child deserved to live no matter how she came to be.

As I was beating myself up inside with regret, my husband appeared with the firewood. He got a warm fire started as night fell and we sat next to each other watching the waves hit the beach.

Max felt a million miles away from me. There was no connection happening and things didn't seem to be going like I had hoped. While my husband was putting out the fire on the beach, I quickly entered the tent, changed into my black negligee, and sprayed some of his favorite perfume. Max came in unmoved by it all, laid down next to me, and fell fast asleep.

I started to cry quietly. The realization hit me hard that there would be no working things out. He was so angry and seemed far away. I just wanted and needed peace and forgiveness. I decided to stop being selfish and making this all about me and think of him. I remembered the pain in his eyes when I told him I was with child, pregnant with his brother's baby. He jumped in the car driving like a lunatic and lost control crashing into a tree. He spent the next four days in a hospital bed with a bad concussion. I believe the Lord allowed him to crash, as I really think that he would be spending life in prison right now. He was out of his mind with fury.

While he was asleep, I changed into my sweatpants and t-shirt. I got up before the sun rose to sit on the beach and confess my sins to the Lord. I poured out my heart to Jesus. I stopped begging for my will to be done and asked for God's will only. I gave up my hopes and dreams right then and there. It felt incredibly freeing.

Max woke up and checked the fish net and yelled, "We caught a fish, Nora, come look!"

We shared a meal together and I sat a healthy distance away. My husband could tell that something had changed, and he seemed to open his heart some. He felt the pressure was gone to not disappoint me. He hated to hurt others. I told him how sorry I was for the affair, and I knew now that he could not be with me anymore. I explained that I had come to accept that. I begged him to forgive his brother. I said it's not worth losing your best friend. His brother, Mark, was so heavily burdened and in a deep depression. He could barely function besides working. He was not the fun easy-going man he once was. Sin steals so much.

I told him I don't deserve it but asked again if he would forgive me. I told him I wanted to be free and that the anger he held was still bonding us together. I explained he also deserves to be free from the chains of unforgiveness. I thanked him for loving my daughter and providing for her the first two years of her life. It amazed me that he never treated her any differently than our girls. I told him I wanted to let him go completely now. I asked him if he would pray with me to do that, and he agreed. We held hands and I prayed, "Lord, please heal our hurts and our hearts. Please bless the ending of this marriage. Give Max the love he has always deserved and please help me to be the mom my kids need. Help him to forgive me and his brother. Please bring complete reconciliation to all involved, and for us as we navigate life apart. Amen."

As it turned out, our story wasn't one that was considered a "true" success story. We returned and gladly accepted our paid for divorce. But for me, it was the greatest success story yet. Max and I began a healing journey and worked on a friendship. We attended counseling to learn to co-parent. He agreed to keep his niece, my daughter, every other weekend with our two girls so she did not feel left out. He reconciled with his brother. His brother was able to forgive himself and I was able to forgive myself. I was able to move on from the pain of shame and regret and once again focus on my relationship with Jesus. I even started back to college and finished my degree as a divorce counselor. I realized a divorce counselor is needed as much as a marriage counselor. I wanted to walk people through the steps to successfully divorce, forgiveness, and co-parenting effectively. Max met a wonderful woman who I believe is truly the best stepmom in the entire world. She is amazing to all my kids. She communicates so well with me. We even meet once a month now for coffee. I consider her one of my closest friends.

After I finished my degree, I offered my services to Revival Island. I would counsel those who chose to go through with the divorce. I saw firsthand Romans 8:28 in action, that God truly does work all things together for good! The Judge accepted my offer, and I happily joined the Revival Island Team. What a win!

Chapter 3

Rig and Riley

The next couple to experience the island was Rig and Riley. Riley was an independent somewhat neurotic woman who had overcome many adversities. She grew up in an abusive home with an alcoholic dad who often beat her mom. She learned quickly how to survive, to appease to avoid physical abuse. She learned how to use humor as an escape and how to keep everyone at arm's length. She felt that her life was so out of control as a child that she tried to control every aspect of it now, including other people. She was in her fifties before she was in a serious relationship and fell in love. Rig was a self-employed, loving, easy-going man. His first wife left him for another man, who was twenty years his junior. He grew up in a home with a controlling, strong-willed mom, and an unavailable dad. Rig was a true pushover. These two unlikely individuals met when Riley needed work done on her house and she was given his name by a friend. Riley was adorable with natural black curls that framed her face. She had olive-toned skin with beautiful green eyes and dimples. She was in the gym every day and a real knockout. Rig could not resist her and won her over with his kind heart.

They had an average marriage the first two years, but years later found themselves exhausted and wanting out. They had grown to resent one another. They could not even stand to be in the same room together. When they were given the opportunity to go to Revival Island, they both said no. The judge asked them to think about it over the weekend and reconvene first thing Monday morning.

Monday at court, Riley had a change of heart. She was a bit of a perfectionist and hated any kind of defeat, so she decided to take this chance. Rig, being a follower, reluctantly agreed. For his items, Rig chose binoculars, a frying pan, an ax, pepper spray, and a tent. Riley chose a notebook, a pen, matches, a water purifier, and a blanket. She planned to journal this experience.

Day one, they decided to set up shelter near the coconut trees. They would look for fresh water in the morning. They didn't speak to each other more than a few words. As soon as night fell, they went to opposite sides of the tent. Riley had the warm blanket and Rig covered himself with tree branches and tried to fall asleep. All he could think of was how sick and tired he had grown of Riley. All she ever did was complain about him, about life, about everything. She was such a negative person. She was always putting him down and trying to boss him around. He thought back on how emasculated he felt when she corrected him, especially in front of others. She always had to be right even when she was wrong. He could not even bare to look at her. She wanted to lead the family and be in charge. He was sick of being someone's little bitch. He wanted out. He prayed that God would give him the strength to complete this week on the island. Then the divorce would be paid for and happen as soon as they returned home. One thing he had was faith in Jesus and he just knew Jesus was on his side. Riley refused to open her heart to the Lord. This also brought contention and separation in the marriage. Rig felt justified to leave the marriage as the Bible says not to be unequally yoked. He was sure the Lord would help bring an end to this soon.

As the sun shone through the crack in the tent, Rig woke up abruptly. The dream he was having felt so real. It was about Riley; she was a little girl and he saw her shaking in a corner. He even saw her little pink nightgown that was covered in orange and yellow balloons. He felt such love and empathy for her in the dream. She looked so scared, little, and vulnerable. Riley looked to be about four years old. She was hiding from her dad who was drunk and beating up her mom. There was blood on a tan sofa and the bathroom floor. He wondered if he had made up the dream from the stories he had heard. He wondered why he had the dream and if Jesus was trying to soften his heart for her. He just had to know if she had a nightgown like that.

"Good morning, Riley. How are you feeling? Did you sleep well?"

Riley rubbed her eyes and sat up. She was not sure how to respond. She couldn't even believe what she was hearing. Rig had not spoken that much to her in years.

"Umm, good morning to you. I did sleep some, but I wouldn't say well." She paused, "How about you?"

"Well, funny you should ask; I did sleep well, and I even had a dream. I was wondering if you had a pink nightgown with yellow and orange balloons on it? I think Jesus gave me a peek into your past. I had a dream you were shaking in a corner, wearing that nightgown. There was blood on a tan couch and on the bathroom floor."

Riley froze in disbelief. How could he know that? She had never shared about that night. It was the worst night of her life. She thought back at what happened. She described how she saw blood and was shaking, hiding in the corner in her favorite balloon nightgown. Her dad was in a drunken rage. He was more violent than usual. He accused her mom of cheating on him when he found out she went across the street to borrow flour from the neighbor. She explained how she was so afraid that she had even wet her pants. She really thought her mom was going to die. When her dad saw the puddle on the floor, he came over to attack her. Her mom jumped up in her defense. She got in the way, and he smacked her so hard that blood from her mouth splashed onto the pink balloon nightgown.

"Rig, it was the worst night of my life. I cried myself to sleep that night and, in the morning, I threw my nightgown away. To even look at it, brought such anxiety."

Rig felt an urging in his spirit to ask if he could hug his wife.

"Riley, can I hold you for a moment?"

Riley did not respond. Rig decided no matter what she would say he would take the initiative and the lead. He went over and gently put his arms around her. She laid her head on his shoulder and cried softly.

"I cannot believe you saw that in the dream," she responded.

"Honey, I believe Jesus wanted me to see that, to understand you better, and to soften my heart again. I had grown so cold towards you. I am so very sorry. Words cannot express how sorry I am that happened. I would do anything to change that night so you wouldn't have had to endure it. Do you want to talk about it? Even if your mom would have died when she jumped in the way to protect you, it would not have been your fault. I think what happened that night caused a lie or stronghold to come into your life."

"I felt so guilty as my mom couldn't open her mouth for days. He hit her so hard when he was swinging at me. I decided right then I would be perfect. I would never pee myself again. I would control my emotions, all my responses, and grow up. At five years old I built a wall around my heart."

"Jesus cried too that night you know. The devil wanted your dad to hurt your mom and to hurt you. And people have free will to make choices. God did not want that to happen."

"Why did He let it happen? Why didn't He stop it?"

"He did intervene. In my dream the police broke in. Did it happen that way, Riley?"

"Yes, the pizzaman had an incorrect address and was at the door bringing a pizza. When he saw the blood and heard the crying, he called the police."

"Honey, that was Jesus. He intervened to stop it, so your mom wouldn't die, and so you wouldn't have to live with that burden the rest of your life. Who knows, maybe the pizzaman was an angel!"

"Oh my gosh, maybe he was. We did try to find him to thank him and could never even get his name. We called all the pizza shops in town, and no one knew who he was. I never even thought of that. I had forgotten that part of the story all along. I focused on the other, the accident, my mom's jaw, the fear, the blood. It shaped me to not trust men, even Jesus, and to rely on myself. But you know what, it was the turning point in my life and my mom's. My dad was charged with assault and forced into anger management classes. He had to live away for a year until he completed the classes and community service. He even started in AA and became sober. That awful day started our path to freedom. Thank you, Jesus, thank you! I see it clearly now. I see how You did help us. I cannot believe I forgot that was the day we became free and safe. Please Lord, forgive me for blaming You. Please, I want to know You. I want a different life. I want to relinquish control. I give You my life. Amen."

I sat stunned at what just happened. I was given a window into my wife's past and felt compassion, love, and understanding for her. Who I despised only moments ago, I now felt connected to and had a new understanding of her. And my wife who tried to do everything herself, had now asked Jesus into her heart. Wow! What is this place?

We ventured out of the tent together and decided to sit and watch the waves. We didn't want to lose this moment. For breakfast, we only had coconut and drank coconut water. We didn't even feel hunger, just warmth and love.

Riley leaned her back against my open legs as we watched the waves crash in. The sky was the most beautiful sapphire blue. The warm sand underneath us felt soft and inviting. As she scooted her backside closer to my front, my body responded. I took the lead, and as I gently pulled her blouse off, she turned to face me. She began kissing me like she couldn't get enough. Before I knew it, we became one again. The feeling was euphoric. We continued to make love and hold each other all day long. I traced the lines of her back, her breasts, her hips, and thighs with my finger. I wanted to remember every inch of her. Oh, how I had missed her.

At the end of the day, we went back to our tent. We slept naked wrapped in the blanket together. We talked half of the night, and the other half slept in each other's arms. When morning came, we decided we needed to find the fresh water and catch a fish. We unfolded the map and began our hunt. It took us four hours to find the water. Luckily, to catch a fish took less time. We chopped firewood and made a beautiful fireplace surrounded by large rocks we found lying around the beach. We cooked the fish in our frying pan and enjoyed a delicious meal of our own making. We worked so well together as a team. Our love felt stronger than ever. I guess Jesus wasn't done with us yet.

Riley journaled our experience. She said this is one memory she never wants to forget. The entire seven days went so fast. We wanted to slow the time. We tried so hard to just sit and listen to the waves and not talk. We were rarely successful, as we had years to make up for. We prayed together every night and, in the morning, sang praises to Jesus. We had so much to be thankful for.

We went to the scheduled appointment with the judge and explained we did not want a divorce but wanted to renew our vows. So instead of a divorce that day, we had a ceremony! We were asked if we wanted to join the team with Amalia and Quin to help in the judge's quest to save marriages. We gladly agreed. The judge said we were her favorite success story so far, as we didn't waste time solidifying our commitment.

We invited Amalia and Quin over for dinner the following Sunday. We shared our experiences on the island and went over ideas on how to create a more successful experience. We decided what was needed more than anything was to cover the island with prayer. We planned to go on two trips a year just to pray over the island and the program and sing praises to God. We decided to make pamphlets and to take pictures of each couple before and after the experience. It would help us to keep track of the progress and notate the successes and failures. We also would commit to praying over the couple's pictures, as a point of contact.

Quin and I became fast friends. We realized we had so much in common as we were both huge sports fans. We started a weekly men's Bible study that met at The Pancake House on the edge of town on Saturday mornings. Our first study was how to be the spiritual leader of the home. Riley and Amalia hit it off too. Every time they were together, they giggled like schoolgirls. They both had an incredible sense of humor and, I think, made it into a competition of who could be the funniest. They met up once a week for prayer and pasta.

We are so beyond grateful that we were blessed to experience Revival Island! The definition of revive per the Merriam-Webster dictionary is to return to consciousness or life: become active or flourishing again. This new program does more than just revive marriages, it provides the tools for them to thrive!

Chapter 4

Martha and Mikey

After careful consideration and after the program was fully functional, we realized some couples have limitations and would not be able to forage around for food and shelter. We wanted this program to be available for them as well, so we put in cabins on the left side of the island. The cabins sat facing the ocean and included air conditioning, two massage chairs facing a beautiful stone fireplace, deluxe mattresses with Egyptian cotton sheets, and a silk comforter. They also included a temperature-controlled hot tub, stove, and stocked refrigerator including immune-boosting smoothies, fruits, veggies, and delicious premade meals and desserts. We wanted the couples to be as comfortable as possible. We understood besides the emotional turmoil this fractured relationship brought, there was also the physical trauma of a health crisis. We spared no cost and had a nurse and counselor in a small trailer on the island. There was also a trailer with a spa and two professional massage therapists and a trailer with a chef to create romantic dinners.

The first couple to qualify was Mikey and Martha. Martha was diagnosed recently with stage three cancer. She was a twenty-nine-year-old and was three months pregnant. Mikey was devastated and even though he had always wanted to be a dad, he wanted her to terminate the pregnancy. For her to carry full term could possibly mean a death sentence. The pregnancy hormones cause cancer cells to grow more quickly, and she would not be able to have the necessary drugs to treat the cancer. Although they had a loving marriage for the last three years, they found themselves in court for a divorce. Mikey was stressing her out so much about her decision to have the baby that Martha had to get away from him, as stress alone could accelerate the cancer. Mikey did not want the divorce but agreed to it as he could not stand watching her die, feeling responsible.

Martha sat in court in a light yellow and gray dress and black dress shoes. Her belly was just starting to show. She looked so sad and nervous yet had a glow about her. She believed the pregnancy was a gift to her and was a great distraction from the cancer that was raging havoc on her small-framed body. It represented hope and life while she faced darkness and uncertainty, staring death straight in the eyes. She immersed herself into the pregnancy with classes and support groups. She had every book written about pregnancy and baby development. She was determined to be prepared for everything and to be the best mom she could be for the time she had. She also had a naturalist's doctor and a dietician. One stressor they didn't have was money. Martha came from wealth and made a great living as a nurse practitioner. Mikey was an accomplished defense attorney. He had his own practice that worked to free those wrongly accused. They were great people that found themselves in a terrible predicament. So, if any couple qualified for the program, they did! It was created for this type of situation. They already had a great marriage and foundation, they just needed to work on communication and acceptance. They were strong believers as well and very active in their church.

The judge walked in, everyone stood up. "Please be seated. After reviewing all the documents provided for the divorce, it's the court's decision at this time to deny this divorce."

This was the first couple to have their divorce denied without first agreeing to the Revival Island.

"This divorce will be allowed if you agree to one week on Revival Island. If you go and still want the divorce, it will be immediately granted and will be free of charge. You would stay at the resort part of the island; all your needs would be provided for you. You would be our first couple to experience this newest program."

Mikey immediately spoke, "Your honor I am not comfortable with a week without medical care for Martha. I will have to decline."

Judge Lilly responded, "The island will have a nurse on site and a helicopter will be on call if any emergency would arise. Also, a counselor will be provided as well to help you work through this very complex situation."

Martha responded next, "I would love to go, Your Honor."

Mickey took a little convincing but agreed to go. Therefore, it was set for three weeks out. This would give the team enough time to get everything in place, for a dietician to create the meals, the massage therapists to be available, and the nurse to go over Martha's medical chart. And most importantly time for the team to go and pray over the island.

Mikey and Martha arrived first-class on a private plane. Waiting as they arrived, was the massage therapist and counselor to introduce themselves and show them around. Also on the island was a trailer that housed a small restaurant with a personal chef to provide their dinners. They were both in awe and blown away. Immediately there was a strong connection as each had desperately missed the other and did not want the divorce. They just felt there was no other way.

They were handed an itinerary. There was counseling at 10:00 AM, a massage at 3:00 PM and dinner started at 5:00. The rest of the day was free time. Martha was overjoyed to have this second honeymoon. As sad as she was that they found themselves in court for a divorce, she was so happy for this second chance to make things work.

Martha spoke first, "Baby, I love you so much. I have missed you with all my being."

She handed Mikey the newest sonogram. Tears welled up in his eyes as this was the first time he found out the sex of the baby. It was written on the sonogram, *'baby boy,'* which was determined by a blood test.

"Oh honey, a boy? We are having a little boy?!? I am so happy; I have always wanted a son! Thank you, Jesus! I am so very sorry I wanted to end the pregnancy. Can you ever forgive me? I just cannot forgive myself if something happens to you!"

"Babe, it's not up to you when I leave this earth and it is not your fault. The Lord allowed us to have a beautiful gift before I go on to eternity. Neither of us knows how much time we have left. We just have this moment, so we need to enjoy our time. I have hope that I will be healed, and I am enjoying every day."

They arrived at 1:00 PM and took time to unpack. They decided to take a blanket and picnic basket that was provided for them. It was packed full of every cheese imaginable, crackers, and plump ripe chocolate-covered strawberries. Instead of wine, there was sparkling juice. They looked so forward to some time on the beach to catch up. They had missed each other the last six weeks they had been apart. They both could not keep their hands off each other. The whole 'absence makes the heart grow fonder' was most definitely the case for them.

This was a perfect day; the temperature was $77°\,F$ and a small breeze filled the air. Mikey spread out the blanket, laid out the crackers and cheese on the beautiful platter, cracked open the juice, and poured it into the crystal wine glasses. This was like a fairy tale. The wind blew through Martha's beautiful blond curls, which framed her perfectly rounded face.

"You are so gorgeous" Mikey beamed! I can't take my eyes off you. I am such an idiot to have almost let you go! This has worked! I don't want to lose you. I want to call the judge and cancel the divorce."

"Mikey, I don't want to lose you either. I want to live all my days with you like my vows stated. But we have things to work through. We need to complete the entire process and then decide. One thing I know is I love you; I love you more now than the day I met you."

They thought back to that day. They met in the most unconventional way. Mikey's doctor was out for surgery, so Martha was seeing his patients. Their eyes locked and the world stopped. It truly was love at first site. Martha pushed it aside and tried to remain professional. Mikey was being seen for a rash all over his hands, arms, and back. The rash ended up being poison ivy. It was the best doctor's visit Mikey had ever had and he didn't want it to end. The cream healed it immediately, but Mikey came in for a recheck. Then he came in once a week for the next two months. He made up issues and had been poked and prodded more than anyone had ever been before. He had every test under the sun and was given a complete good bill of health.

Mikey had no other reason to come in, so he had to bite the bullet and ask Martha out. He could not think about anything else. Martha was elated and that began their six months of dating which quickly led to a huge elegant, beautiful wedding. The three years that followed were a marriage full of joy, until the night it all came crashing down. Martha was driving home after a long day of working a double shift, passed out on the drive, and crashed into a field. Luckily, a passerby saw and called 911. When Mikey was notified, he rushed to her side. The hospital ran tests and found her to be dangerously anemic. After a blood transfusion and more tests, the diagnosis was cancer and pregnancy. They were devastated and happy if you can be those two things at once.

After more tests and the cancer growing quickly, Mikey decided the baby had to go. His wife, his love, needed to abort to get the necessary treatment so they could have more time together and a chance at remission. Martha was not on the same page and would not hear of it. A wedge quickly grew between them, and they could not even bare to be in the same room. Mikey moved out quickly to the small room that was above his office. They stopped communicating as Martha could not share anything about the new miracle growing in her body. It angered and sickened Mikey. He grew to hate the little baby growing inside.

But now on the island and knowing the sex of the baby, Mikey had a change of heart. He was willing to support his wife in her decision and work to keep her stress as low as possible. They made sure to go to counseling every day on the island. They made great headway. Mikey was determined not to be overbearing and Martha agreed to work part-time and complete conventional treatment after the birth. They were able to compromise and openly discuss their feelings and fears.

Mikey also decided he needed to be strong and to share his fears with a trusted friend and counselor. He needed to remain positive as Martha was in a fight for her life. The time on the island was a major success. They had made so many memories. They spent the mornings enjoying coffee on the ocean, the afternoons napping in the comfortable bed, and the evenings at the couple's massage. They had fancy dinners enjoying lobster, steak, fettuccini, and the best homemade rolls, so sweet and salty, dripping in freshly cured butter.

They arrived at court at 8:00 AM the morning after leaving the island. They both ran up to the judge's chamber and before they were asked said, "Your honor, we want to stay together!"

The judge could not contain her joy and burst into tears. She ran down to them, and they all embraced in a hug. She said they were the reason she designed this program. They were the couple she wanted to save, those in a situation out of their control who felt desperate and thought that divorce was the only answer. She said if she only saved their marriage, it would have all been worth it. After that news, she took the day off to celebrate.

Martha delivered a healthy baby boy. The cancer had not spread any further and after giving birth she immediately started a more aggressive therapy, which included chemotherapy. It was the one thing she had promised to Mikey that she would do. She responded incredibly to it and remission was a real possibility in the very near future!

They sent a thank you card to the judge with the words, "We are forever grateful the Eternal Judge cared enough to give us a second chance through the workings of an earthly judge in a place called Revival Island."

About the Author

Kim Foulkes was born in Peoria Illinois. She is the youngest of two daughters. She is a proud mom and grandma of six beautiful girls, with another on the way. Kim has worked the last twenty-two years for an insurance company. Her most rewarding job was doing home daycare when her children were young.

Kim has had a lot of difficulties in her life, mostly due to her own poor choices. She has worked hard to face the pain and to work through the healing. She wanted to make a better life for herself and for her family.

Kim felt compelled to write a book that reflects her true belief in the sanctity of marriage. Although she has faced multiple divorces herself, she believes marriages that are free from abuse are worth fighting for. She has seen beautiful examples of marriages throughout her life, through her parents and some very close friends. She loves to see marriages thriving.

Kim started an online Christian support group for survivors of narcissistic abuse. Another group she started with a friend is called, The L.E.A.P. Room. L.E.A.P. stands for Love, Encouragement, and Prayer. She is a beautiful friend to many and has walked their paths with them.

Kim makes sure to include others in her daily prayers. She is a true prayer warrior revealing her heart's desire to love others and to lead them to the love of Jesus.